Little Ant
and the Snail

S.M.R. Saia

Illustrations by Tina Perko

One day, Little Ant was scurrying back to the anthill with a very large crumb when he passed a snail heading in the same direction. Little Ant had never seen anything so slow, and he stopped to have a better look.

"Do you always move so slowly?" Little Ant asked the snail.

"You don't have to be fast to get things done," the snail replied.

"You have to be fast to do things more than once," Little Ant said, "or to do more than one thing at a time."

"Maybe," said the snail. "But I am content to do one thing today and to do it well, however long it takes me."

"I am starting to outgrow my shell," the snail explained. "I heard there is a pretty one at the end of this field, and I am going to go and move into it."

"Not if another snail gets there first,"
Little Ant said.

"I'll get there sooner than you think,"
the snail answered. "If you want, I will
even race you there."

"There is no way that you could beat me in a race," Little Ant said. "I am far quicker than you. I would easily win. You would only embarrass yourself."

But the snail said, "Being fast isn't everything," and continued on his way.

Little Ant was so irritated at the snail for not appreciating his speed that he decided he would teach the snail a lesson.

"I will race you," Little Ant said. "I will race you, and I will win, and then we will see how important it is to be fast."

Just then a beetle walked by. Little Ant stopped him. "This snail and I are going to run a race," Little Ant said, and the beetle laughed.

"Will you please fly to the end of this field and draw a finish line in the dirt? You can be the judge of who crosses the line first." The beetle agreed. "Tell every insect that you see about the race," Little Ant told the beetle as he flew away. Then he turned to the snail. "You will wish that you, too, were fast when you see everyone cheer for me."

"Suit yourself," the snail said.

Little Ant picked back up his crumb.

"I will bring along my crumb, so I don't have to come back for it," Little Ant told the snail. "Plus, you will see that it is good to be able to do more than one thing at a time."

His crumb on his shoulder, Little Ant crouched at the starting line, bobbing up and down a few times to stretch his muscles.

"Are you ready?" he asked the snail.

"I'm ready."

"One, two, three, go!"

Little Ant took off running, and soon the snail was far behind him. Little Ant was very pleased. He thought the snail and his "do one thing slowly and do it well" plan was silly.

He was about halfway to the finish line when he spotted another crumb, even bigger than the one that he was carrying.

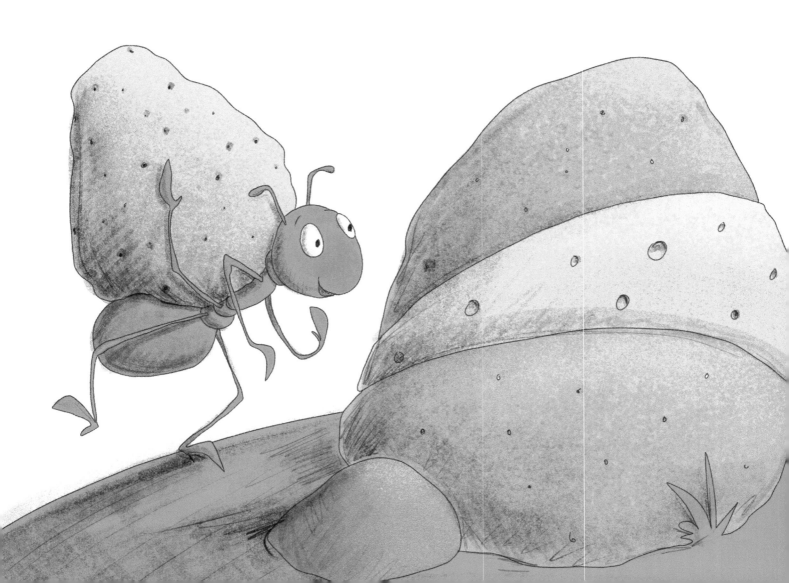

He was going to exchange his crumb for this even bigger one when he had a better idea.

"I will bring back both crumbs," Little Ant decided. "When the snail finds out that I crossed the finish line carrying two big crumbs, he will have to admire me both for my speed and because I can do more than one thing at a time." So Little Ant picked up the second crumb and set off again.

But this time he didn't run. Why should he? The crumbs were heavy, the day was hot, and the snail was still far, far behind him.

"I can walk to the finish line and still beat the snail," Little Ant said to himself smugly.

He walked on until he found yet a third, even bigger crumb. Little Ant was beside himself with glee. "I will also bring this third crumb," he decided.

Little Ant started off again, but three crumbs were very heavy, and he struggled to keep his balance. He found himself walking more and more slowly in order to keep from losing his crumbs. "It doesn't matter," he told himself. "I am so much faster than the snail that I will certainly still win this race."

To prove it to himself, he turned to look over his shoulder to see if the snail was anywhere in sight. His movement caused his crumbs to get off balance, and before he knew it, all three of the crumbs had fallen off of his back and were rolling and bouncing away from him across the field in three different directions.

Little Ant ran after them. It was no longer enough to just win the race. He had to cross the finish line with his three crumbs!

Little Ant found the first crumb. Then he found the second crumb. Then he went in search of the third crumb.

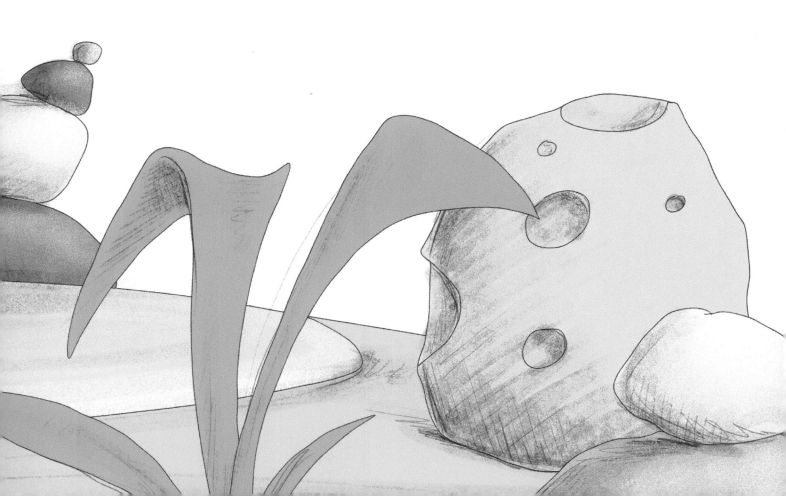

The snail, meanwhile, had continued his slow and steady pace behind Little Ant, following Little Ant's footprints, thinking all the while about the pretty shell that he was going to move into at the end of the day. He was so focused on that pretty shell that he didn't even notice that Little Ant's footprints were no longer on the ground in front of him. On he went.

When Little Ant finally had all his crumbs, he rejoined the race. He imagined himself waiting at the finish line when the snail finally arrived. He imagined the snail admitting that Little Ant was faster and that faster was better.

But when Little Ant saw the finish line, the snail was already there, being cheered as the winner by every insect of the field.

"I should have won this race!" Little Ant pouted.

"You would have won the race if you had focused on winning the race," Uncle Ant agreed. "Never lose sight of what you're trying to accomplish, Little Ant."

An embarrassed Little Ant carried his big crumbs, one at a time, back to the anthill. The snail, meanwhile, moved into his prettier and roomier new home and was very happy indeed.

Copyright 2019 by S.M.R. Saia
Illustrations by Tina Perko

Free activities for the Little Ant books are available at
http://littleantbooks.com.

Follow Little Ant on Facebook at @littleantnews. Learn more about Little Ant's
life; be the first to know when there are new Little Ant activities available for
free download, and get cool news about insects you can share with your kids!

I am grateful to Phoebe Saia for her story development help with this book,
and for designing the colors for the snail's two shells.

Published by Shelf Space Books
http://shelfspacebooks.com

ISBN: 978-1-945713-32-3